Bath Time

In a rundown old mansion perched on a hill there lives a family of stray cats. These cats play music, love parties and live without a care in the world.

MEET

The Nazz

Last Chance

King Tubby

Cheeta

Petal

Mr Clean

Timmy Tom

Thorn

AND

Spook

One day, a small girl with two black pigtails knocks on the cats' front door. Before they know what's happened, she's moved in! The cats have a firm **NO HUMANS** policy, but the girl isn't like regular humans. She wears a bright orange costume with ears and paws and a tail, and she says

'MEOW!'

Not that the cats know what that means.

Her name is **KITTY** – they read it on her collar. It seems all Kitty wants to be is a cat. **But...**

Bath Time

JESS BLACK

LOTHIAN
Children's Books

On the rare occasion when the cats weren't playing music together, they could sometimes be found on the couch watching their favourite TV shows. One cloudy afternoon, when the rain had forced her inside, Kitty settled in with Spook who was glued to the latest episode of a romantic soap opera.

'I can't believe you watch this rubbish,'
said Thorn, rolling her eyes. She was
waiting impatiently for her own favourite
show to come on next.

'S h h h h !' Spook shushed her, edging
closer to the screen.

Kitty had to agree – Spook's show was pretty boring – but she could tell by the dramatic music that something important was coming up. Just at that moment she was distracted by a tickle in her throat.

'Hack, hack!' she coughed.

'Shhhh!' shushed Spook again.

Kitty tried hard to hold the cough in, but she could already feel another one coming on.

'HACK! HACK!'

'Kitty,' groaned Spook, 'please stop interrupting!'

Kitty didn't mean to. She didn't know why she was suddenly coughing so much, but she slipped out of the lounge room anyway to leave Spook in peace.

Later that day, Kitty found The Nazz, Cheeta and Timmy Tom jamming in the music room. She picked up a microphone, ready to join in with some improvised lyrics.

As Cheeta finished off a guitar solo with a twang, Kitty took a deep breath and –

'Hack!'

Timmy Tom jumped, sending the jingle jangle of his tambourine out of time with The Nazz's piano notes.

Kitty tried again. **'Hack!'**

'Is she trying to beatbox?' Timmy Tom asked, glancing at the others.

13

'Kitty, please, you're really throwing off our groove,' Cheeta said.

'Hack!' Kitty coughed.

'I don't like the sound of that,' said The Nazz.

'Yeah, Kitty,' Timmy Tom agreed, 'you're a little off-key.'

'HACK! HACK! HACK!'

was all Kitty
could reply.

The Nazz suggested they call a house meeting to get to the bottom of Kitty's strange cough. Kitty tried her best not to interrupt, but the tickling at the back of her throat was worse than ever.

'I think our poor Kitty has a cold,' said
Petal.

'Well, that's easily fixed,' piped up Mr Clean.
'Put **three goldfish** in warm water
and gargle twice daily.'

Gargling goldfish? Kitty wasn't so sure about that. She tried to swallow but another cough almost escaped.

'I don't think that would help, Mr Clean,' replied Petal. 'If Kitty's got a cold, she'd have a human cold, and that needs human medicine.'

'Correct!' said King Tubby. 'And as usual, I have just the thing.' He held up an enormous book. 'We'll find everything we need to know in King Tubby's

Giant Encyclopaedia of Medical Maladies.'

He heaved the book open to a random page. 'Let's see. First, we should check her beak temperature. Is she having any difficulty flapping her wings? I think we need a feather sample.'

Thorn glanced over King Tubby's shoulder. 'Tubby, that's a book about bird watching.'

Just then, Kitty coughed her loudest cough yet:  'HAAAACCCKKKKK!'

Out came two balls of fur.

Instantly, she felt better and could go back to licking the back of her hands like the cats had shown her.

'Fur balls!' said The Nazz. 'Who has been teaching Kitty to clean herself?'

All the cats raised a paw.

'And has *anyone* taught her how to clean herself *like a human*?' The Nazz asked.

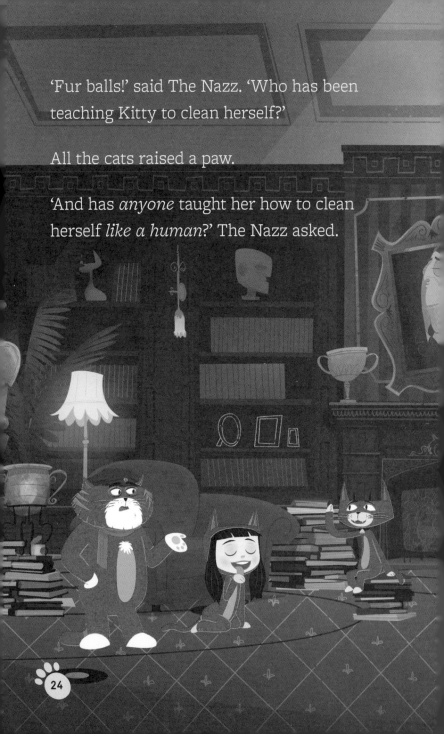

'How are we supposed to know how humans clean themselves?' Thorn retorted.

'Actually,' said King Tubby, 'I believe they have special rooms just for that. *Bath*rooms. They wash themselves *and* go to the toilet there.'

'Ew!' said Timmy Tom, horrified.

'Using *water*,' King Tubby continued.

'EW!' cried all the cats, shuddering at the thought.

'You know what, I think this house might have one of those special rooms,' said The Nazz.

The cats looked at him, wide-eyed.

'Well, come on,' he said. 'It's high time Kitty cleaned herself like a human!'

The bathroom was the only room in the whole house that the cats never entered. The door had been firmly shut for as long as anyone could remember.

'I have a bad feeling about this,'
said Spook, shaking at the thought of what
lay behind it.

As The Nazz pushed the door open, it gave a long, low creak. The cats stuck their heads around the door cautiously. No one wanted to be the first to go in.

Kitty reached for the light and stepped inside.

Before them was a dusty, damp room covered in cobwebs.

33

'Don't touch anything!' warned
The Nazz as he approached a tall plastic
curtain on the far side of the room.

But the others weren't listening.

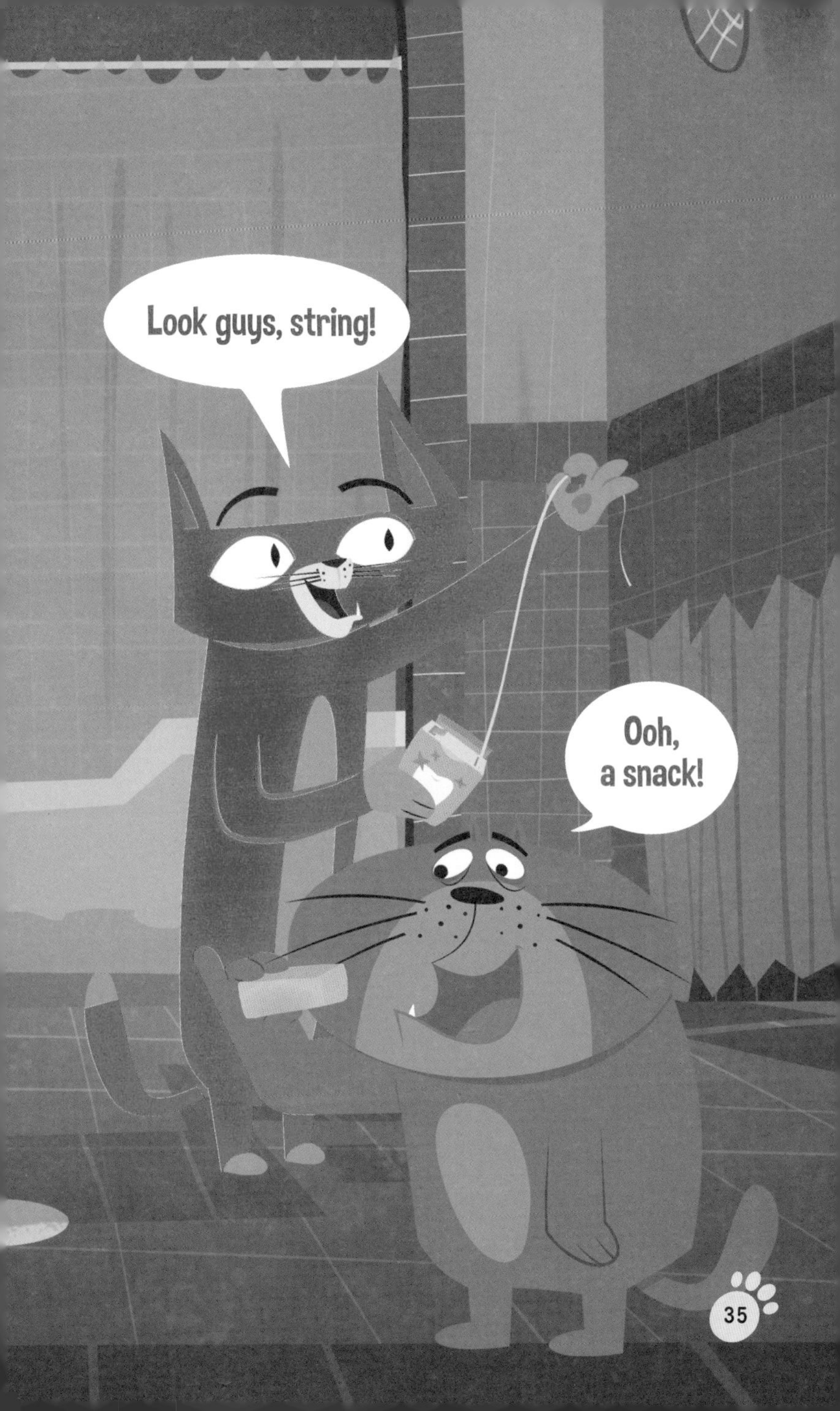
Look guys, string!
Ooh, a snack!

Kitty couldn't help laughing at the cats' curiosity, but she knew The Nazz wasn't going to be distracted. He took hold of the plastic curtain and tugged. Behind it was a bathtub that didn't look inviting at all. No way was Kitty getting in there.

'This must be where they wash themselves!' The Nazz announced.

The other cats bounded over.

'How does it work?' asked Timmy Tom.

Kitty could have explained, but if the cats didn't know then they couldn't make her use the bath. She hung back behind Timmy Tom.

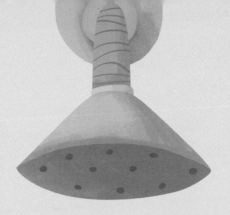

'Isn't it obvious?' King Tubby was saying. 'The water comes out of this **thingumajig**, which is connected to this **what's-it**, and the what's-it is connected to this **doodad**. So, if my calculations are correct –'

As he turned the
tap there was a loud
CREAK and **THUD** and

WHOOSH!

A powerful jet of freezing cold water shot out of the shower. It was so strong it knocked King Tubby off his feet and out of the bath.

'Well done, Tubby!' said The Nazz.
'Now, Kitty, hop in!'

Kitty took a step back. 'Meow, meow, meow!'

'Maybe you need a demonstration.' The
Nazz looked around. 'Any volunteers?'

The cats scampered away, leaving Mr Clean by the bath. Reluctantly, he stepped in, the dirt in his fur turning the water a dark brown.

Well, Kitty certainly wasn't getting in *that*. It was now or never.

She bolted for the door.

It was clear she wasn't coming back. The cats realised that if they couldn't get Kitty to the bath, they'd have to get the bath to Kitty.

First, they tried putting a bucket of water above a door to catch her unawares, but she was too fast and the bucket missed her.

Next, they tried leaving a tub of water
at the bottom of the bannister, but
Kitty sailed right over it.

Then Cheeta suggested throwing water balloons,

but Kitty sent them flying right back at the cats.

Finally, The Nazz tried reasoning with her.
He found Kitty hiding up one of the trees
in the garden.

'Now listen, kid –' The Nazz began, but before
he could continue, a loud **SQUEAK**
came from the window of the neighbouring
house. **SQUEAK**. They heard it again,
followed by splashing and giggling.

For Kitty, it was the unmistakable sound of someone playing in the bath with a rubber duck.

'Meow!' she said, delighted at the thought.

'Wait a second,' said The Nazz, finally realising what all this was about. 'Kitty, would you enjoy a bath more if you had a rubber duck to keep you company, too?'

It turned out that Timmy Tom made an

excellent squeaky bath-time buddy.

Later that night, a squeaky-clean Kitty sat with The Nazz as he played a tune on his piano.

'Humans have some very strange habits, Kitty,' said The Nazz, 'but as **wet** and **runny** and despicable as water is, I have to admit – it must be nice not to get fur balls.'

Kitty couldn't agree more. It felt good not to have that tickle in her throat. Bath time had been so much fun, and now she felt **warm** and **cosy** and ready for bed.

Just then, The Nazz let out a loud **HACK** and a giant orange ball of fur landed on the piano keys with a clang.

Kitty and The Nazz looked at each other – and burst out laughing.

'Now, that's making music!' said The Nazz, and he raised his paw like a conductor.

Kitty knew her cue. She held a microphone close to her mouth and sang. They were back to making music together.

COLLECT THEM ALL!

KITTY is not a CAT
Lights Out!

KITTY is not a CAT
Teddy's Bear

KITTY is not a CAT
Hired Hound

KITTY is not a CAT
Bath Time

A Lothian Children's Book
Published in Australia and New Zealand in 2020
by Hachette Australia
Level 17, 207 Kent Street, Sydney NSW 2000
www.hachettechildrens.com.au

10 9 8 7 6 5 4 3 2 1

 A catalogue record for this
work is available from the
National Library of Australia

ISBN 978 0 7344 1979 8

Cover and internal design by Liz Seymour
Cover and internal illustrations by BES Animation
Printed and bound in China by 1010 Printing